I1002585

Rotary 1993
Melbourne Australia

Dear Tyler S Morgan,

This is a story about some of our native animals and some of the different types of food we enjoy in our country. We hope you enjoy it.

From
Thomas (4), Sarah and Henry (2) Brunskill.

BUSH PARTY

For Anastasia, Tala and Dana

Bush Party

Tricia Oktober

HODDER AND STOUGHTON
Sydney Auckland London Toronto

Gecko loved his
corner of the bush.
It was his garden.
One day he decided
to have a party
in his garden.
Then all his friends
could enjoy it too.

You are invited to a party at Gecko's garden on the first Tuesday in November at 1 o'clock.

Please wear your most beautiful hat, and bring a plate of food.

Your friend,
Gecko lizard.

So he sent out special invitations.

All the bush creatures
were so excited!

Some chattered for hours about the hats they would wear.

Others wondered what
all the fuss was about.

On the day,
guests looked splendid
in their fine spring hats.
Most had been specially
made for the occasion.
There were flowers and
ribbons, caps and parasols,
handbags and jewellery.

Butterfly arrived
late of course
but everyone agreed
she looked magnificent.

The food was delicious.
There was pavlova,
fairy bread, lamingtons,
trifle and, of course,
chocolate crackles.
Everyone had plenty to eat.

Some ate a little too much!

The bush rang
with laughter
at Galah's magic tricks.

But all was hushed
when the acrobats
balanced expertly.

When Gecko chose
the most beautiful hat
there was resounding applause.
The winner nervously
accepted her prize.

All too soon
it was time to go
and Gecko
reluctantly
said goodbye.

That evening
the bush filled
with the sunset calls
of the animals,
praising Gecko
and his beautiful garden.

' First published in 1986 by
Hodder and Stoughton (Australia) Pty Limited
10-16 South Street, Rydalmere NSW 2116

Limp edition 1990
Reprinted 1991, 1992

© Tricia Oktober, 1986

This book is copyright. Apart from any fair dealing for the purpose of
private study, research, criticism or review as permitted under the
Copyright Act, no part may be reproduced by any process without
written permission. Enquiries should be addressed to the publisher.

National Library Cataloguing-in-Publication entry
Oktober, Tricia
Bush Party.
ISBN 0 340 49611 8
1. Title
A823'.3
Typeset in 30/33pt Century Light by Dovatype, Melbourne
Printed in Hong Kong by Colorcraft Ltd.